Sister Magic

Mabel Makes the Grade

BY ANNE MAZER

ILLUSTRATED BY BILL BROWN

SCHOLASTIC INC.

New York Toronto London Auckland Sydney
Mexico City New Delhi Hong Kong Buenos Aires

To Susan Weber Tranchina
and her third-graders

No part of this publication may be reproduced, stored in a
retrieval system, or transmitted in any form or by any means,
electronic, mechanical, photocopying, recording, or otherwise,
without written permission of the publisher. For information
regarding permission, write to
Scholastic Inc.
Attention: Permissions Department
557 Broadway, New York, NY 10012

ISBN-13: 978-0-439-87248-5
ISBN-10: 0-439-87248-0

12 11 10 9 8 7 6 5 4 3 2 1   7 8 9 10 11 12/0
40

Printed in the U.S.A.
First printing, November 2007

Chapter One

It was the first day of school. Mabel stood in her room with a long list in her hand. As she read each item, she checked it off.

"New paper, new folders, new erasers, new backpack. Check," she said.

"Books read over the summer, listed in alphabetical order. Check," she said.

"Sharp pencils, lined up by color in new case. New box of crayons. Check," she said.

"'What I Did on My Summer Vacation,' parts one, two, and three. Check."

"Hair brushed and tied back with ribbon. Face washed. Nails cleaned. Teeth brushed. Check."

"White blouse, plaid kilt. Check. Day-of-the-week underwear, Monday. Check."

She sighed with satisfaction.

Mabel was ready for third grade. Just like she was always ready for everything.

This year, her teacher was Mrs. Worthing. She was an old-fashioned, strict teacher who gave plenty of homework. She demanded good behavior from her students.

Mabel had heard that Mrs. Worthing never gave perfect report cards, but Mabel was determined to get one.

This year, Mabel was going to get not only straight A's, but straight E's for effort, cooperation, and attitude.

"E" was for excellent.

Mabel intended to be the best student in the class.

The door opened. Mabel's little sister, Violet, walked into the room.

"I got dressed up for kindergarten," she announced.

Mabel stared at her in dismay.

Violet wore a lime polka-dotted shirt, aqua pants, pink socks, and tangerine high-top sneakers with blue laces.

Her hair was combed in the front, but not in the back.

One hand had nails with sparkly orange nail polish. The other had bright purple nails.

Violet looked like a bag of brightly colored Halloween candy. Or like a package of Magic Markers had exploded.

And Mabel had to walk her to school.

Mabel glanced at her watch. There was still time for Violet to change.

"Shall I help you pick out another shirt?" she offered.

"I like this shirt," Violet said. "It's beautiful."

"Maybe plain sneakers," Mabel suggested. "They'd look so nice."

"I don't think so," Violet said.

"Blue socks to match your pants?" Mabel coaxed.

Violet shook her head.

Mabel silently counted to ten. Then she picked up her brush.

"What if I just fix your hair? It's a little tangled in the back." Mabel edged closer to her sister. "You don't want nasty snarls, do you?"

"Snarls are good," Violet insisted.

"Oh, never mind," Mabel said angrily. She threw the brush on the bureau.

The two sisters went downstairs.

Their mother was waiting in the living room. She had a digital camera in one hand and a wad of tissues in the other.

"It's Violet's first day of kindergarten," she said. She blew her nose loudly. "My baby is all grown up."

Violet jumped up and down. "I'm five!" she yelled. "I'm grown up!"

"I'm so proud of you both," their

mother continued. "Mabel, you're absolutely perfect."

Mabel beamed. She worked hard at perfection.

"And Violet, you look so *cute*!"

Mabel sighed. Violet didn't work at anything. She just did what she wanted.

And cute?

It wasn't the word *she'd* use to describe Violet.

Words like *messy, loud, annoying,* and *crazy* came to mind when she thought of her little sister.

Their mother snapped a couple of pictures of Violet, then stopped to blow her nose again.

She picked up the camera and pointed it at Mabel.

"Smile!" she said as her eyes filled with tears. "It's the first day of school!"

Mabel tried to look happy for her mother.

She loved school. But this year, Violet was going, too.

Mabel had to walk to school with someone who was dressed like a box of crayons.

Not to mention that Violet interrupted people, said strange things, and didn't listen.

And not to mention that Violet had magic.

Mabel tried not to think about it, especially on the first day of school.

She just hoped that Violet would keep her magic where it belonged — at home, in her room, in the dark, and utterly secret.

Mabel wondered if she could pretend that Violet was someone else's little sister.

She was ready for third grade, but she wasn't ready for Violet.

Chapter Two

"Do you remember the rules I taught you?" Mabel asked as they walked down the front steps.

"Rules? I know all about rules," Violet said. "Brush your teeth after meals. Eat everything on your plate. Don't throw food at people."

"Those are family rules, Violet. I'm talking about school rules."

Violet bit her lip. "Um, share toys?"

"Sure," Mabel said. "Do you know any others?"

"Say your A, B, Please!"

"ABC's," Mabel corrected. "And that's not a rule, Violet, that's *learning*."

"Oh," Violet said in a small voice. She took Mabel's hand. "Does kindergarten hurt?"

"No, Violet," Mabel said. "Kindergarten never hurts."

She patted her little sister's hand reassuringly. Violet was only a little girl scared of her first day of school.

"You'll be fine," Mabel said.

Violet looked relieved.

"Remember," Mabel said. "Line up at the door when the bell rings before school.

Get a pass to go to the bathroom. Raise your hand when you want to talk."

"Line up at the bathroom rings," Violet repeated. "Raise the door when the bell gets a pass."

Mabel sighed. "Just listen to your teacher, Mr. Bland. He'll tell you everything you need to know."

"I will," Violet promised.

"Good." Mabel took a deep breath and said a word of encouragement to herself.

She suddenly felt very nervous, as if she were the kindergartner and Violet were the third-grader.

What she had to say wouldn't make Violet feel better. But it would make Mabel feel a *lot* better.

"Violet, you have to promise me . . . no magic in school. *Ever*."

"Okay, Mabel," Violet shrugged.

"No blackbirds flying out of pies. No toy horses galloping around the room. No Frisbees changing direction in midair."

"No, Mabel." Violet counted them off on her fingers. "I won't do any of those things." She smirked.

"You have to be careful, Violet," Mabel said in her most serious voice. "Imagine what could happen if your magic got loose in the school."

"What?" Violet asked with interest.

"Something really bad." Mabel didn't want to scare her little sister too much . . . or did she?

She imagined what would happen if Violet's magic got out of control. There would be trips to the principal's office, staring classmates, and angry conferences with parents.

Violet would be the most notorious kid in the school. And Mabel would never live it down.

It would *ruin* her life.

Mabel chose her words carefully.

"If Mom found out," she said, "she'd be *so* upset."

"I understand," Violet said. "No magic at school. I promise!"

She sounded like she meant it.

Mabel squeezed her little sister's hand. Even if Violet wore crazy colors and didn't comb her hair properly, sometimes she wasn't half bad.

Chapter Three

"Hey, Mabel! Violet! Wait up!" Mabel's friend Simone ran toward them. Her black hair was braided around her head. Her eyes gleamed behind pointy blue glasses.

"Are you excited about your first day of school, Violet?" Simone asked.

"Um, sure." Violet chewed on a strand of hair.

"Don't worry. In a few years, you'll be brave and confident," Mabel said. "That's what happens when you get to third grade."

Mabel felt brave and confident, especially now that Violet had promised not to do magic in school.

Simone leaned in close to Violet. "Did Mabel warn you about the crossing guard?"

"Crossing guard?" Violet looked confused.

Simone winked at Mabel.

Mabel took up the joke. "He waits for the kindergartners," she said in a hushed voice, "and then . . ."

Violet's eyes widened in alarm. "And then *what*?"

"He . . . he . . ." Mabel stopped, as if she couldn't bear to go on.

Violet let out a small cry.

"He gives everyone a pencil," Simone said quickly. "Sometimes he hands out balloons, too."

"Will he let me choose my favorite color?" Violet looked relieved.

"Of course," Simone said.

"Scared you, didn't we?" Mabel couldn't resist teasing Violet a little more. "Ha-ha."

Violet scowled at her older sister. "I'm not afraid of anything!"

"I saw you," Mabel gloated.

They were crossing the street. Mabel lifted her foot to step over the curb. She stumbled and lost her balance.

Next thing she knew, she was on the ground.

Simone gasped. "Are you okay?"

"I'm fine." Mabel got up slowly and dusted herself off. "Nothing's hurt."

Except her pride, of course.

Mabel glanced back at the curb. It was the same curb as always. She'd stepped over it hundreds of times.

But something wasn't right. She had never tripped like that before.

Had Violet . . . ? Mabel shook her head.

She had just promised not to do magic.

Mabel was just imagining things.

Suddenly the curb shimmered blue. Then it returned to its normal concrete self.

Mabel stared hard at her little sister.

Violet wouldn't meet her eyes.

"You've got to lift your foot *over* the curb, Mabel," Simone teased. "Not walk into it."

"Yeah, Mabel," Violet chimed in. "Don't be afraid of a silly curb."

Normally Mabel would have blushed. Or she might have made a joke out of the whole thing. But she wasn't embarrassed or laughing now. She was angry.

"You made a serious promise," she reminded Violet.

"What serious promise?" Simone asked.

She couldn't tell Simone about the magic. She couldn't tell anyone. Why did Simone have to butt in? "To follow directions and to, um, listen to her teacher," Mabel said.

Simone looked at Mabel like she was crazy. "No one goes into kindergarten knowing *any* rules," she said. "Give her a break!"

"I want her to have a head start."

"You worry too much, Mabel." Simone linked her arm through Violet's. "Our Violet will learn everything she needs to know."

Violet stuck out her tongue at Mabel. "Ha-ha," she said.

I shouldn't have teased her, Mabel thought. *But* she *shouldn't have done magic.*

She sighed. She was just going to have to forget about it.

And she would, as long as it was the *last* magic she saw today.

Chapter Four

Mabel sat up very straight with her hands neatly folded in front of her.

Her teacher, Mrs. Worthing, stood in front of the class with a piece of white chalk in her hand.

Her hair was cut short and severe. She wore a gray tailored blouse, a pearl necklace, and gray slacks. On her feet were gray moccasins.

"This is what I expect for the beginning of the school year," Mrs. Worthing said. "First, a five-subject notebook."

The other students scrambled for papers and pens. Only Mabel sat quietly.

She already had a five-subject notebook.

"An essay on your summer vacation, due at the end of the week," Mrs. Worthing continued. "No longer than five pages and no shorter than three."

Mabel had already written her essay. It was four and one-half pages long.

"Be sure to check for grammar and spelling," Mrs. Worthing said.

Mabel had done it.

"And I expect neat handwriting in black or blue ink."

That went without saying. Mabel would

never turn in a paper in pink, bronze, yellow, or silver ink. And her handwriting was always perfect.

"In addition, you need to read three chapters of this book by next Monday." Mrs. Worthing held up a paperback novel.

Mabel had already read it.

Third grade was off to an excellent start.

"Why aren't you writing anything down?" the girl at the next desk leaned over to ask her.

"I've already done it all," Mabel replied.

The girl's eyes widened. "Wow," she said. "How did you do that?"

"Preparation," Mabel said, with a modest shrug.

"Don't you wish we had Ms. Toby?" the girl said.

"No," Mabel said.

Ms. Toby was the other third-grade teacher. She liked to sing in class. She wore white tunics and baggy pants in crazy colors.

Her class sat in a circle instead of in rows. They had "centering time." They didn't get grades, they got personal growth reports.

Mrs. Worthing didn't do any of that.

But she wasn't a bad or mean teacher. She was strict but fair. She had high standards.

And if anyone could meet them, it was Mabel.

She was up to the challenge.

Mrs. Worthing put down her chalk. "Does anyone have any questions?"

There was a brief silence in the room.

"Good," Mrs. Worthing said. "Now we're going to have a quiz."

The class groaned.

"You won't be graded on it," she said. "Not this time. I want to see how well you read and write."

The girl rolled her eyes. "See?" she said. "I told you."

"Don't worry," Mabel said. "It doesn't count toward your grade."

Mabel took out a piece of paper and a dark blue pen.

Mabel loved school. She loved tests. She loved hard work and strict teachers.

In school, you knew one plus one always equaled two.

The letter *C* always came after *B* and before *D*. It couldn't suddenly decide to sit next to *Z* or *M* or *Q*.

If you got a wrong answer, the teacher took off points. If you knew all the answers, you got one hundred percent or an A+.

School was safe and predictable. Mabel loved it because she always knew what was coming next.

Chapter Five

"There are my girls! How was your first day of school?" Their father was behind the counter, waiting on customers.

He beamed at Mabel and Violet.

"I got everything right on Mrs. Worthing's quiz," Mabel told him proudly.

"Congratulations, pumpkin," her father said. "I knew you could do it. What about you, Violet?"

"I got lost on the way to the bathroom," Violet said.

Mabel gazed at her sister in alarm. "You did?"

"The janitor found me," Violet continued. "He showed me a secret shortcut through the cafeteria. The cafeteria lady gave me a banana."

"You had quite an adventure," her father said.

"My teacher, Mr. Bland, has a mustache," Violet said. "When are we getting ice cream?"

"Soon," her father said. He punched numbers into a computer. "That'll be ninety-eight dollars, with the discount," he said to a customer.

"I'll be with you in a minute," he said to Mabel and Violet.

"Take your time, Dad. Violet and I will check out the new sweaters." Mabel had noticed them on her way into the store.

"I don't want to check out the new sweaters," Violet said.

"Sit here, then." Mabel pointed to a wooden bench.

"No."

Mabel sighed. "Do you want to play school? I'll be the teacher."

"You *always* get to be the teacher."

"Just this time," Mabel said. "Please?"

"Oh, all right." Violet flung herself down on the bench. "Give me some homework."

Mabel stepped across the aisle. "Name the colors of these sweaters."

"Yellow, red, orange, white, green, blue," Violet recited.

"Good job, class." Mabel touched the soft knitted fabric and congratulated herself for being so clever. "Now count the colors."

"One, two, four, three . . ."

"Four comes *after* three," Mabel corrected.

Maybe Dad would bring one of the sweaters home for her — if she could decide which color she liked best. They were all so beautiful.

Her smile faded. The sweaters were moving. Sleeves were twisting and turning and reaching upward.

Mabel whirled around, hissing "Violet!"

Her little sister sat on the bench, swinging her legs. "What?"

"Stop it!"

The sweaters continued their dance.

"You promised you'd play school with me," Violet said.

"Oh, all right," Mabel said.

The sweaters collapsed. They flopped on the table, all in a tangle.

Mabel hurried to straighten them out.

"You don't need to fold the sweaters,

pumpkin." It was her father. "Things get messed up fast around here."

"It's okay, Dad," Mabel said. She glanced over at Violet. Her little sister was counting stripes on underwear.

She wanted to say, "Violet's magic did it." But she couldn't.

Once, not too long ago, she used to tell her father everything. But she had promised her mother never to speak of magic to *anyone*.

Magic ran in Mabel's mother's family. She hated and feared it. Maybe Mabel's mother was a tiny bit ashamed of it, too. So no one else knew about the magic, not even Mabel's father.

Mabel wished she didn't have to keep secrets from her father. But a promise was a promise.

She had to keep it.

Now her father reached into his pocket and took out a five-dollar bill.

"This is for ice cream," he said. "Go treat

yourselves. I'm too busy to leave the store right now."

"All right, Dad," Mabel said. "I'll take good care of Violet."

"I know you will," her father said. "That's my girl."

Chapter Six

As soon as they were out the door, Mabel turned on her sister.

"How many times do I have to tell you? No magic. Especially not in Dad's store."

Violet opened her mouth to speak, but Mabel didn't let her.

"Get this through your head," Mabel said. "No excuses, no reasons, no magic, *ever*."

"But, Mabel," Violet protested. "I just did what you said."

Mabel stared at her little sister.

"I kept my magic in all day at school. Wasn't that good of me?"

"Um, yes, it was, Violet," she admitted.

Mabel remembered all the instructions she had given Violet this morning. Her first day of kindergarten couldn't have been easy.

Hadn't Violet followed the most important rule of all? She hadn't done any magic in school.

So what if she did a little magic in the store? Mabel suddenly thought.

That magic was harmless. Maybe it even let off steam.

Mabel had folded the sweaters right back up. No one was the wiser.

Mabel took a deep breath. "I'm proud of you, Violet," she said. "You did something very, *very* good today. You didn't use your magic in school."

Violet beamed. "Now I get ice cream."

"Anything you want," Mabel said. "Tell me what else you did in school today."

"Sang songs. Played with blocks. Made finger paintings."

"That sounds like fun," Mabel said. "What did you like best?"

"Singing," Violet said. She began to warble a tune.

Her voice was off-key, but Mabel smiled at her little sister as they entered the ice-cream store and went up to the counter.

"May I help you?" the woman behind the counter asked.

"I'll have a small vanilla cone," Mabel said. "With chocolate sprinkles."

"I want raspberry, pistachio, and bubble gum ice cream in a waffle cone," Violet announced. "And rainbow sprinkles, too."

Mabel put the five-dollar bill on the counter. The woman shook her head. "You need another dollar and five cents."

She searched in her pockets and came up empty. "I guess we'll have to have our ice cream without sprinkles," she said to Violet.

"You *promised*."

"Yes, but I don't have enough money." Mabel knelt down to explain things. "You're a big girl now. You can have ice cream without sprinkles, just like me."

Violet made a face. "Plain ice cream. Ugh."

"Here it is." The woman handed the girls their cones. Both had sprinkles.

For a moment, Mabel felt confused. Maybe she hadn't ordered right? What did she do now?

The woman frowned. "I don't remember giving you those sprinkles," she said. "And I know for sure that you didn't pay for them."

Mabel's face turned red. "I . . ."

"Your father won't be happy if I tell him you snuck sprinkles."

"We *didn't*!" Mabel cried. She looked at Violet. "Did we, Violet?"

Her little sister had rainbow sprinkles on her face and a pleased smile.

"Violet?" Mabel repeated.

Violet licked her cone.

"Kids today have no respect," the woman said.

Mabel held out the ice-cream cone. "You can have mine back."

"You touch it, you buy it," the woman said.

"I don't have *any* money," Mabel protested. She thrust a hand into her empty pocket, just to make sure.

Her fingers touched something cool and round. It was a quarter. There was another one, too. Suddenly her pocket was full of coins.

She glanced at Violet. Her hands were sticky. Bubble gum ice cream dribbled down her chin.

"Here." Mabel tossed a handful of quarters onto the counter. "Is this enough?"

"You had the money after all," the woman said in disgust. "Just trying to get something for nothing. I know kids like you."

Mabel grabbed Violet's arm and fled the store.

"Violet," Mabel said when they were safely down the street.

"Moolf?" Violet mumbled.

"Um, well . . ." Mabel didn't know whether to scold her or to praise her. "Thanks," she finally said.

Violet didn't answer. She was too busy eating ice cream.

Mabel took a lick of her cone. The magical chocolate sprinkles were delicious.

Chapter Seven

The first bell had just rung. Mabel slid into her seat. She breathed in the school smells of chalk, blackboards, and schoolbooks.

Then she glanced at her morning list.

Fresh notebooks and sharpened pencils. Check.

Library books in bag. Check.

Shirt tucked in. Check. Socks pulled up. Check.

Mabel sat up straight, ready for a new day at school.

Mrs. Worthing clapped her hands for attention. "Are you ready for a little test?" she asked.

"So early in the morning?" a boy said in dismay.

"This one will be fun," Mrs. Worthing promised. "We're going to test how well you see."

"Are we going to visit the eye doctor?" someone said.

Mrs. Worthing ignored the comment. "This is about your powers of observation," she said. "How carefully do you notice things? Look around the classroom, everybody. Who sees something different?"

Mabel's hand shot up. She wanted an A+ for observation.

But she didn't see anything different in the room. It was exactly the same as yesterday.

"Is it the flag?" she asked hopefully.

Mrs. Worthing shook her head.

"Are there more math books on the shelves?" Mabel guessed. "Do we have new chalk for the blackboard?"

"No more wild guesses, Mabel," Mrs. Worthing said. "Pay attention."

Simone's eyes sparkled behind her pointy blue glasses. "I know, Mrs. Worthing."

"Yes, Simone?"

"The walls are freshly painted."

Mrs. Worthing smiled. "Excellent, Simone."

Mabel slid down in her chair. Of course. Why hadn't *she* seen that?

Mrs. Worthing continued. "Who knows what a mural is?"

Simone's hand went up. So did Mabel's.

"Simone?" Mrs. Worthing said.

"It's a painting on a wall," Simone explained.

"That's what I was going to say, Mrs. Worthing," Mabel said.

"Good." The teacher smiled at both girls.

"Now let's see a show of hands," she said. "Who'd like to paint our classroom walls?"

This time almost every hand in the class shot up.

Mrs. Worthing looked pleased. "Guess what, third-graders! We're going to paint a mural in our classroom!"

An excited murmur spread through the classroom.

Mabel glanced at the girl who didn't want to be in Mrs. Worthing's class. Maybe she was changing her mind right now. This was as much fun as anything that Ms. Toby's class did.

A boy raised his hand. "Are we going to paint all four walls?"

"The *entire* room," Mrs. Worthing said. "Just imagine, our mural will be here for years and years to come. Generations of third-graders will see it every day. This is a great honor. We each have to do our very best work."

Mabel sat up very straight. She unclasped her hands and then clasped them again. These were the words she had been waiting to hear.

Mabel was going to do her *best* "best" work on the mural.

Her paintbrush would never drip. Her colors would never clash. She would always stay inside the lines.

"I need volunteers," Mrs. Worthing said.

Mabel's hand shot up.

"Just a second." Mrs. Worthing smiled at her. "Wait until you hear what you're volunteering for."

Mabel kept her hand up. Mrs. Worthing

needed to know that she'd volunteer for *anything*.

"Don't be so eager," Simone whispered.

"Why not?" Mabel whispered back. "Mrs. Worthing will remember who raised her hand first."

"Maybe," Simone said. "But, on the other hand, maybe not."

"She knows I want to help," Mabel insisted.

Simone shrugged. She never seemed to try too hard. And yet top grades and awards always came to her.

It was practically magic. No wonder she hit it off so well with Violet.

Mrs. Worthing stepped up to the blackboard and began to write. "I'll need people to help with supplies, sketching, and paints."

Mabel stretched her arm up as high as it would go. It all sounded good to her.

"All right, Mabel, since you're so enthusiastic, I'm going to give you a special job."

"Yes, Mrs. Worthing." Mabel cast a triumphant look in Simone's direction. *"See?"* she said under her breath.

"I'd like you to be our volunteer coordinator."

"Of course, Mrs. Worthing." Mabel didn't know what a volunteer coordinator was, but it sounded important.

"I'll explain this job to you a little later," the teacher said.

Mabel nodded. Mrs. Worthing wanted her to do a job. She was going to do it well. That was all that mattered.

Chapter Eight

Mrs. Worthing picked up a piece of chalk. "First, we're going to make a list," she said.

"Lists! My favorite thing!" Mabel exclaimed.

She had notebooks at home that were filled with lists. Her father joked that Mabel made lists even as a baby.

Mrs. Worthing printed some words on the board and underlined them: "'<u>What We Do in School</u>,'" she said.

"This is the subject for our mural," the teacher announced. "Who has ideas?"

"Me!" Mabel cried. "We do reading and writing."

"Very good, Mabel," the teacher said. She wrote it down on the blackboard.

Her idea was number one, Mabel noted with satisfaction.

"Pledging allegiance," Simone said. "Studying outer space. Making baking soda volcanoes."

"Eating lunch in the cafeteria," a boy said. "Games at recess. Solving math problems."

"Playing soccer in gym class," a girl said. "Riding on the school bus."

"Raising hands to talk," someone else said. "Going to the library. Learning about other countries."

"Excellent," Mrs. Worthing said. "These are all wonderful ideas."

Mabel smiled proudly, as if the ideas had all been hers. "When do we start, Mrs. Worthing?" she asked.

"Very soon," the teacher said.

Simone raised her hand. "Can we paint anything we want?"

"You're going to work in small groups. Each group of students will decide which school scene they want to paint."

Mabel wondered what kind of scenes would most impress Mrs. Worthing.

A book tea? A science fair? A portrait of the teachers? She hoped her group would come up with an outstanding idea.

Mrs. Worthing continued. "And I have another surprise for you."

"Ice cream?" a boy said hopefully.

"A field trip?" asked someone else.

"I've invited some children from the other classes to help us. This mural is not just for us. It's for the entire school. The younger children will enjoy it when they get to third grade." Mrs. Worthing glanced at the door. "The guest artists will be here shortly."

Guest artists? Mabel thought. *Why not?* It sounded like fun.

The teacher turned to Mabel. "Mabel, as our volunteer coordinator, you'll be in charge of helping the guest artists."

"I *love* to help out, Mrs. Worthing."

Mrs. Worthing nodded.

The door opened. A group of younger students filed in.

"Welcome, guest artists," Mrs. Worthing said. "Thanks for being part of our mural project."

Mabel smiled at them. She was going to be the most enthusiastic volunteer coordinator that Mrs. Worthing had ever seen.

"Mabel, raise your hand so that everyone knows who you are," the teacher said. "Does everyone see Mabel?"

"Yes," the guest artists said.

"She's here to answer your questions and help you out. I'll explain more in a minute."

"You can ask me anything," Mabel said.

Mrs. Worthing nodded approvingly.

The door opened again.

"One more guest artist!"

There was a blur of bright tangerine sneakers, striped aqua pants, and a polka-dotted pink T-shirt.

Violet skipped into the third-grade classroom.

Chapter Nine

"Oh, *great*!" Simone said. "Violet is here. How lucky is that?"

How un*lucky is that*, Mabel thought. She buried her head in her hands.

"Hey." Simone nudged Mabel. "What's your problem?"

"Will our volunteer coordinator please come to the front of the class?" Mrs. Worthing said.

Mabel stood up slowly.

She should have felt happy and important. She should have felt excited and pleased.

But she didn't.

It wasn't fair. Her classroom was her private haven. It was the one place where she didn't have to worry about her little sister or her magic.

How *dare* Violet come in here?

"Nooooo," Mabel groaned.

Mrs. Worthing was talking to the guest artists. "Mabel will show you where the supplies are. She'll help you find smocks to protect your clothes. She'll fetch drop cloths to put on the floor. She'll answer questions if I'm busy."

I will have to answer Violet's questions, too, Mabel thought miserably. Her visions of being a volunteer coordinator had *not* included her sister.

But she made herself smile at the kids. "Does anyone have questions for me?"

Violet raised her hand.

Mabel suppressed another groan.

"Why am I here?" Violet said.

Some of the kids in Mabel's class snickered.

Mabel rolled her eyes. Of all the dumb questions!

"Mabel?" Mrs. Worthing said.

"You volunteered," Mabel said.

Violet looked confused. "Vol-um-what?"

Mabel sighed. "You're going to help us with our mural." She took a breath. "A mural is a painting on a wall. We're going to paint these walls with pictures of school life."

Violet's eyes lit up. "Can I finger paint?"

"No, we'll use brushes," Mabel said. "Anything else?"

The other kids were silent.

Mabel looked at Mrs. Worthing. "Okay, Mrs. Worthing?"

"Thank you for an excellent explanation, Mabel," the teacher said. "You can sit down now."

"Way to go," Simone said as Mabel slid back into her seat. "You were great. And isn't Violet adorable? She's just so cute!"

"Mmm," Mabel said.

Mrs. Worthing rapped on her desk. "Now we're going to divide into groups of three or four students. Each group will include a guest artist."

"I hope Violet works with *us*," Simone said.

Mabel stared at her in alarm. "No way," she said.

"But she's your little sister!"

"Exactly," Mabel said.

She suddenly noticed flickering colors on the empty walls. Mabel squinted at them. Were they some kind of reflection? A sun catcher maybe?

The colors sharpened. A school playground appeared on the wall. Kids ran across it. And then the kindergarten teacher, Mr. Bland, showed up. He wore a polka-dotted bow tie and a cardigan sweater.

Oh no, Mabel thought.

A first-grader broke the silence. "Awesome."

"It's the latest technology," a third-grader whispered.

"I've already got one," someone else bragged.

Only Mabel knew they didn't.

No one had it. No one could buy it. And no one could stop it.

Except for one person.

Chapter Ten

Like everyone else in the room, Violet was staring at the pictures on the wall.

Mabel inched toward her. Her heart pounded.

Had the teacher noticed? She was writing names of groups on the blackboard.

Mrs. Worthing put down the chalk for a moment. "You're very quiet and well-behaved today," she said to the class.

Mabel was almost close enough to give Violet a little shove. Would that break the spell?

"Sssst," she hissed.

Violet jumped. The pictures on the wall faded and then vanished.

Simone appeared at her side. "Did you see that, Mabel?"

"The chalk?" Mabel babbled. "I love writing on the blackboard, don't you?"

Simone gestured impatiently at the wall. "Not the blackboard, silly!"

"What?"

Simone's lips quivered. "Stop playing dumb. You know what I'm talking about."

"Simone and Mabel, pay attention," Mrs. Worthing interrupted. "You're going to be working together. I'm assigning you a guest artist."

"Oh yes, Mrs. Worthing!" Mabel cried. "I can't wait!"

"I expect you to cooperate and help each other."

"Of *course*, Mrs. Worthing."

"Come here and meet your new third-grade friend," the teacher said to one of the guest artists. "Mabel and Simone, this is . . ."

"Violet," said Violet.

Mabel turned pale. Or maybe she turned

red. She couldn't breathe. She thought she might even faint.

This was *way* too close for comfort, especially when magic was happening.

Mabel hoped that Violet had just forgotten her promise for a moment.

But even if she never did magic again in school, the damage had been done.

Simone had noticed. And maybe others had, too.

"Violet!" Simone cried. "Hooray!"

"So you already know each other," Mrs. Worthing said.

"Of course," Simone said. She looked at Mabel as if to say "What are you waiting for?"

"Um, she's my sister," Mabel stammered.

Violet flung her arms around her sister's waist.

"I see," Mrs. Worthing said. She studied them for a moment. "Is it okay to put you two in the same group?"

Mabel wanted to say "No, it isn't." She wanted to tell Mrs. Worthing that having Violet in her group was the worst idea ever.

She wanted to beg her to send Violet back to kindergarten.

But she couldn't say a word. Not with Mrs. Worthing looking at her like that.

Mabel wanted an E for effort, cooperation, and attitude. She didn't think she'd get one if Mrs. Worthing knew how she really felt.

Simone spoke up. "We'd love to have Violet on our team!"

"Good," Mrs. Worthing said. "That's settled."

Chapter Eleven

After supper that night, Mabel went up to Violet's room.

"Come in!" said a muffled voice.

Mabel opened the door. She blinked rapidly.

Violet's walls were orange, pink, red, and turquoise. The curtains were green; the bed was polka-dotted.

It had been that way for a while, but Mabel still wasn't used to it.

Violet was pasting autumn leaves on colored paper. "I'm doing homework," she announced proudly.

"Kindergartners have homework?"

"I'm making a college."

"You mean a *collage*," Mabel corrected her. "A college is a school. A *collage* is an art project."

"I *know*," Violet said. She picked up a bright red leaf and twirled it by the stem. "It's a leaf college."

"*Collage*."

"College."

"Whatever." Mabel sat down on her sister's polka-dotted bed. "Violet, you broke a promise today."

"Sorry!" Violet pasted another leaf onto her paper.

"You're sorry?" Mabel repeated. "That's it? You did magic in *my* classroom!"

"I didn't mean to, Mabel." The autumn leaves on her desk fluttered as if a breeze had blown through them.

Mabel hugged her shoulders. It was unexpectedly cold in the room. "Is there a window open?"

Leaves began to drift down from the

corners of the room. They blew along the floor and skidded under the desk.

"What's going on?" Mabel said. "Violet?"

Her little sister shrugged. "Nothing. I'm not doing anything."

Autumn leaves began to pour from the ceiling.

In only a moment, the room was buried. Leaves covered the floor, the bed, and the bookcase in deep drifts.

Mabel couldn't see her feet anymore. She couldn't see the desk. She couldn't see Violet.

"Stop it!" she cried. "Turn it off!"

"I don't know how!" Her little sister's voice sounded faint and distant.

Mabel jumped up in a panic. She stumbled in the heavy downpour of leaves. Her heart pounded frantically.

"Violet!" she cried. "Where are you? Are you okay?"

"Boo!" Her little sister jumped out from a pile of leaves.

"Violet!"

A few stray leaves drifted to the floor. The storm was over.

Mabel collapsed on a chair in relief. "You scared me," she said.

"Sorry," Violet said. She had leaves stuck in her hair, in her clothes, even in her ears. "I didn't mean to, Mabel."

"If you don't *mean* to do magic, why do you?"

"It just happens sometimes," Violet said in a small voice.

"Those pictures on the wall today?"

Violet nodded.

Mabel wanted to scold her sister. But then suddenly she remembered her own first days in kindergarten. She had felt confused and out of sorts. When she came home, she was so cranky that she had thrown her favorite doll at the wall.

Maybe that was what was happening to Violet.

Except that it involved magic.

For the first time, Mabel was glad that Violet was in her group. She was going to have to keep a close eye on her.

If Violet couldn't control her magic, Mabel was going to have to do it for her. If she could.

Chapter Twelve

"Today we'll meet with our groups," Mrs. Worthing announced. "We'll decide what to paint on our patch of wall."

While Mrs. Worthing talked, Mabel handed out smocks and jars of paint. She was just starting on the drop cloths when the door opened.

The guest artists walked in.

"Mabel, show the younger children how to use a paintbrush," Mrs. Worthing said.

Mabel straightened with pride.

She selected a fat paintbrush. She held it up in front of the guest artists.

"Pay attention, everyone," she said. "You, too, Violet. Dip the brush halfway in

the jar. Take it out. Let it drip for a moment. Then wipe it off very lightly."

Her little sister looked pale and sleepy. Mabel hoped that kindergarten wasn't too much for her.

Mabel thought about the leaf storm last night. What if Violet's magic was exhausting her?

That was something new to worry about.

Mabel unscrewed the cap from a jar of orange paint. She dunked the brush in.

"Oops," she said. She hadn't followed

her own instructions. She had put the brush in too far. It was completely covered with orange paint.

Before she could wipe it off, Mrs. Worthing took the brush from her hand. "That's not how you do it."

"I know, Mrs. Worthing," Mabel said. "I made a mistake." Her heart raced. She *hated* to make mistakes!

The teacher shook her head. "Simone, please explain." She held up the wet brush. "Why isn't this a good idea?"

"If you have too much paint on the brush, it drips on the floor," Simone said. "It dribbles down the mural. It stains your clothes."

Simone glanced at Mabel and shrugged apologetically.

"Thanks, Simone," Mrs. Worthing said.

Violet raised her hand. "Mrs. Worthing," she said. "Mabel did it perfectly one gabillion percent."

"I *didn't*," Mabel said, blushing. Violet

was only making it worse. Mabel wanted to disappear.

Mrs. Worthing nodded at Violet. "It's nice of you to defend your big sister. But you all need to know the correct way to use a brush."

Suddenly Violet snapped her fingers.

Mrs. Worthing stopped in midsentence.

The class sat motionless. The entire room was eerily still. It was almost as if Violet had frozen everyone.

Except for Mabel. She looked around with panicked eyes.

"Unfreeze them!" she hissed. "Now!"

Violet smiled at Mabel. It was almost as if she felt sorry for her.

Then she snapped her fingers again.

Mrs. Worthing blinked and stared. She shook her head. Then, without a word, she handed the paintbrush back to Mabel.

It was completely clean.

"Go on with your demonstration," Mrs. Worthing said to Mabel. "What are you waiting for?"

Chapter Thirteen

"Did you see *that*?" Simone said, rubbing her hands together.

"See what?" Mabel couldn't meet her friend's eye.

"You know."

Mabel tried to look innocent. "No, I don't."

"Did you see it, Violet?" Simone asked.

Violet was counting paint jars. "One, five, three, six, ten," she said, "red, orange, yellow, pink, green. . . . *Nope*."

Simone turned back to Mabel. "Come on, help me out here."

Mabel unscrewed the cap from a jar of

yellow paint and picked up her brush. Her hands were shaking.

Kids weren't supposed to use magic to fix their mistakes.

Ms. Worthing wouldn't like it at all.

"*That* brush!" Simone's eyes narrowed.

And Violet seemed to know what she was doing. If you asked Mabel, her little sister seemed perfectly in control.

Mabel dunked it quickly into the paint jar. They were supposed to be painting a mural, weren't they?

"That brush had too much paint on it, and then it didn't," Simone said slowly. "It was just like, well, magic."

"Don't be silly," Mabel mumbled. She began to outline a girl's head on the wall.

"I'm *not*," Simone said. "And why are you starting the mural without me and Violet? We haven't talked about it yet."

"Let's get going, then," Mabel said. She was more than ready to change the subject. "Tell me your ideas."

"I want to paint pictures of science stuff," Simone said. "You know, baking soda volcanoes, models of the solar system, rocks and crystals. . . ."

"It's a good idea," Mabel admitted. "But I have a better one. An awards ceremony."

"An awards ceremony? I don't get it. *Why*?" said Simone.

"No one else in the class will think of anything like it," Mabel said. "It'll be special, unique, and *very* interesting."

And besides, she thought, *it will give Mrs. Worthing a big hint.* Maybe Mabel would get an award for being the best volunteer coordinator. Or she'd get a good citizen award. Or a most improved award. If Violet didn't mess things up first.

"I guess." Simone sounded doubtful.

"Trust me, Mrs. Worthing will *love* it."

"But we have to talk to Violet first," Simone said. "Right, Violet?"

Violet had stopped counting paint jars. She was cutting out stars from colored paper. "I want to make a Magic Marker mural! I want to draw pictures of Magic Markers all over the wall!"

"No," Mabel said firmly. She refused to do anything with *magic* in its name.

Simone knelt down to Violet's level. "Is there anything you especially like about school?"

"Nap time," Violet replied.

"That's very nice," Simone said, "but only kindergartners take naps. Try to think of something we *all* do."

"What about a nice awards ceremony?" Mabel prompted. "With buttons and ribbons and sashes and certificates."

She glanced at Simone. "An awards ceremony is something we *all* want."

"Well . . ." Violet lopped off the tip of a star.

"You can draw stars on the sashes," Mabel coaxed.

"Red stars?" Violet said. "Orange ones? Blue and purple ones?"

"Whatever color you want."

"Hold on a minute," Simone said. "Don't the science experiments have a chance? We need to vote on this."

"Oh, all right," Mabel said. "But I vote for the awards ceremony. It's a surefire winner."

"I vote for science," Simone shot back. "Violet? You're our tiebreaker."

Violet cut out another lopsided star. She held it up in front of her. "I think . . . I think . . . Do you think this star is beautiful?"

"Oh yes," Simone said. "It's lovely."

"Can I make a star college?" Violet snipped at the paper.

"Coll*age*, no, you can't," said Mabel.

Her little sister closed her eyes.

"Well?" Mabel said. "Get on with it, Violet. What's your decision? Science or awards?"

Violet appeared to be meditating. "I want

the award cereal," she finally said. "With stars in it."

"Hooray!" Mabel hugged her little sister.

"Are you *sure* this is a good idea?" Simone said.

"Mrs. Worthing will love it," Mabel said again. "It's practically guaranteed."

Chapter Fourteen

They had just put the finishing touches on their part of the mural. Now Mabel stood back to admire it.

She had painted a girl standing on a stage. The girl wore a winner's sash across her chest and a crown on her head.

She held a small golden statue. The principal was handing her a scroll with a bright gold seal.

A huge audience, painted by Simone, applauded her. Violet had sprinkled the scene with stars and blue ribbons.

A boy came up to look at the mural.

He squinted as though he'd never seen anything like it before. "Is that the Olympics or something?"

"It's an awards ceremony," Mabel said.

His mouth dropped open. "An a-what?"

"You know, good citizen awards, scholarship awards, that kind of thing," Mabel explained.

"Oh. Yeah. Sure." The boy walked away.

"See?" Simone said. "I told you. No one gets it."

"They do, *too*," Mabel insisted. "He was just a bit slow."

Simone shook her head. *"You* don't get it, Mabel."

"I do, too." Mabel turned to a girl sitting at the next desk. "Do you know what this is?" She pointed to the awards ceremony.

"Of course," the girl said. "It's a play."

Mabel shook her head. "Try again."

"Is it Parents' Night?" the girl asked. "Friday morning assembly?"

"No."

"The *Oscars*?"

"Never mind," Mabel said crossly.

Obviously none of her classmates had ever won an award. Or even wanted one.

"*See?*" Simone said. "See?"

"Wait until Mrs. Worthing gets here," Mabel said. "*She'll* understand."

Simone only shook her head.

"And this is . . . ?" Mrs. Worthing asked a few minutes later.

"An awards ceremony, Mrs. Worthing."

She studied the mural carefully, then pointed to the girl with the golden statue. "Tell me about her, please."

"That girl is a winner," Mabel said to her teacher. She was going to be one, too.

"What did she do?" Mrs. Worthing asked.

"Um," Mabel said. She had forgotten to figure that out.

She thought fast. "It's a general award

for, you know, everything. She's good at everything." *Just like me,* she added silently.

"I see," Mrs. Worthing said. "And whose idea was this?"

"Mine," Mabel said. She paused. Maybe she was taking too much credit. "Simone and Violet painted it with me, of course."

"I did the stars," Violet suddenly piped up. She was sitting on the floor, cutting out snowflakes.

Simone was quiet.

"I see," Mrs. Worthing said again. She smiled at the three girls and passed on to the next group of students.

"Didn't I tell you? She loved it!" Mabel cried.

"Do you think so?" Simone asked.

"How could she *not* love it? It's fabulous." Mabel sighed with satisfaction. "I can't wait to see the prize she gives us."

Simone frowned. "She didn't say anything about a prize."

"You'll see," Mabel predicted. But suddenly she felt uneasy.

She decided to look around at what the others had done. As she studied the rest of the mural, she felt more and more uncomfortable.

There were scenes of the cafeteria, gym class, the library, and the playground. Kids studied, read, ate, and played games.

It was all about daily life in a school.

No one else had done anything like what Mabel, Simone, and Violet had done.

Mabel hurried back to see the awards ceremony again.

Only a few minutes ago, she had loved it. She thought that it was wonderful. But now she saw it with new eyes.

Their mural picture didn't show daily school life. It showed only one girl, alone, getting an award.

Simone had seen the truth. No one got it. Probably not even Mrs. Worthing.

Mabel wasn't going to get an award. She'd be lucky if she got a passing grade.

She groaned out loud.

"What's the matter?" Violet asked.

"It's this mural!" Mabel burst out. "We never should have painted an award ceremony. Simone was right!"

She glanced around. Simone was on the other side of the room.

Mabel was glad. She wasn't ready to admit to Simone that she had made a mistake.

"*I* like it," Violet said. "It's full of stars."

Mabel patted her sister on the head. "Thanks, Violet. It wasn't your fault. You were a big helper."

"I was," Violet agreed.

Mabel paced back and forth. "I just wish that the whole school wasn't going to see it," she said miserably.

"They'll like it," Violet said.

"They won't," Mabel moaned. "It's going

to be on the wall for years and years and *years* to come, until we have great-grandchildren!"

She buried her face in her hands. "There's no way to change it."

"Yes, there is," Violet said. She stood up and pointed her little finger.

Chapter Fifteen

Mabel gaped at the awards ceremony.

It was the same scene, and yet it wasn't.

The girl receiving the award was still there. But now a number of students stood in line to join her onstage.

It was no longer about one girl getting one award. It was about a whole school.

Parents applauded in the audience. Some of them had cameras. There were even a couple of babies.

"It's a graduation ceremony!" Mabel cried. "Violet, you're a genius!" She flung her arms around her little sister.

"I fixed it for you, Mabel."

"You did a *great* job!" She was almost speechless with relief.

Violet might have just as easily changed the awards ceremony into a playground fight. Or into a swimming pool. Or into blackbirds coming out of a pie.

But instead, Violet had done the most perfect thing ever.

Her magic had saved the mural.

She had probably also saved Mabel's grade. *And* Mrs. Worthing's opinion of Mabel.

"How did you know to do a graduation ceremony?" Mabel asked her.

"Natasha," Violet said.

Natasha was their older cousin. Last spring, Mabel and Violet had attended her graduation from middle school.

Mabel wondered why *she* hadn't thought of that.

"Wasn't it a good idea?"

"*Yes!*" Mabel agreed. She made a mental note: From now on, she'd *always* be extra nice to her little sister.

Simone came up beside them.

"This whole mural is fantastic!" she cried, indicating the classroom. "Have you seen . . ."

Her mouth dropped open. For a moment, she couldn't speak. Then she said in a hoarse voice, "What happened to *our* mural?"

"Violet and I touched it up a bit."

"Touched it up?" Simone repeated in disbelief. "*That's* not a touch-up. How could you do that in five minutes?"

"We're, um, fast workers."

Simone fired off questions. "Where are the paints and brushes? Where are the drop cloths? How come your hands are so clean?"

"We washed up and put everything

away," Mabel said. "We wanted to surprise you. Don't you like what we did?"

Simone studied the mural. "It's a lot better now," she admitted. "It's more about what everyone does in school."

"It was *my* idea," Violet announced.

Simone pursed her lips. She seemed about to fire off another round of questions.

But she only said, "Who did the line of kids marching onstage?"

"*Me,*" Mabel and Violet said at the same time.

"I mean, it was Violet," Mabel said.

"It was Mabel," Violet said.

"You're up to something," Simone said. "I wish I knew what it was."

"We're cooperating," Violet said.

"Yes, we *are*." Mabel put her arm around her little sister.

"Mrs. Worthing will like *this* one," Violet said. "We're going to get a good grade."

"Did Mabel tell you that?" Simone had a curious look on her face.

"I just know," Violet said smugly.

"You do, don't you?" Mabel agreed.

Simone shook her head. "I'll never understand you two."

Chapter Sixteen

"Oh my," Mrs. Worthing said. "You've really made this mural so much better."

Mabel beamed. She patted her little sister on the back. "It was Violet's idea. She's extremely intelligent for a five-year-old."

Violet was busy cutting out long curly shapes from paper and sticking them in her hair.

"I mean, *sometimes*," Mabel murmured.

Mrs. Worthing went on. "You've been a great help, Mabel, during this entire mural project. And you've worked well with your little sister. It's not always easy to have a sibling on your team."

Ha! Mabel thought. *If only Mrs. Worthing knew!*

"I'm so glad to have you and Simone in my class this year," her teacher said. "You both have a great attitude. It's going to be a good year."

"It is," Mabel agreed. She glanced at Simone. She hadn't said much to Mrs. Worthing. But she looked pleased, too.

Who would have thought that Violet's magic would be so helpful? Mabel wondered. *Who would have thought that* Violet *could be so helpful?*

She had messed up only a few times. That wasn't very much, was it?

Violet was turning over a new leaf. It opened up possibilities.

There were all sorts of places where Violet's magic might come in handy.

"Class, take out your writing notebooks," Mrs. Worthing said. "Guest artists, wait quietly until your teachers come to get you."

Mabel pulled out a sky blue notebook. A butterfly flitted past her face. She brushed it away.

"We're going to write essays about the mural," Mrs. Worthing said. "What did you learn?"

I learned that my little sister isn't so bad, Mabel thought. *She's actually kind of wonderful. . . .*

Another butterfly landed on her shoulder, then flew off.

Mrs. Worthing continued. "Did our mural project make you think about school in a new way? Did you like working on a team? Painting on the walls?"

Several more butterflies fluttered past the teacher.

"What's this?" Mrs. Worthing said. "Did someone leave the window open?"

Mabel jumped up to close it.

"Thank you, Mabel." Mrs. Worthing picked up a piece of chalk. "You might write about all the people who are going to see the mural. Your friends, parents, and, maybe one day, your *children*."

Butterflies began to swarm in front of the blackboard.

"This is unheard of!" Mrs. Worthing exclaimed. "Has someone's science project escaped?"

Something was wrong. Mabel looked over at Violet.

Her little sister was cutting out butterflies from colored paper.

Her scissors snipped rapidly, releasing one butterfly after another into the air.

Of course it wasn't science; it was magic. Mabel should have known it was all too good to be true.

Butterflies were everywhere. The air was thick with them.

"Oh dear, I better call the janitor," said the teacher, batting them away.

"Don't worry, I'll take care of it, Mrs. Worthing!" Mabel cried. She grabbed a butterfly net from the shelf.

"Stop!" she hissed to Violet.

Violet looked up. "But I'm having fun," she said.

"Violet!"

"Oh, all right." Violet rubbed her nose.

The butterflies began flying straight toward Mabel.

She held up the net. "Gotcha!" she cried.

Mabel ran to the window, opened it, and released the butterflies into the open air.

Mrs. Worthing went to her desk. She

took out a blue ribbon. She offered it to Mabel.

"Thank you, Mrs. Worthing." She proudly pinned the ribbon on her blouse and returned to her desk.

"No more funny business," she muttered to her sister.

A tiny green butterfly flew out of Violet's hair.

"Yes, Mabel," she said.

About the Author

Anne Mazer is a Mabel who secretly wants to be a Violet. She grew up in a family of writers in upstate New York. She is the author of more than thirty-five books for young readers, including the Scholastic series The Amazing Days of Abby Hayes and the picture book *The Salamander Room*. For more information, please visit Anne at her website, www.amazingmazer.com.

Author photo by Mollie Futterman